Dear Parent:
Your child's love of reading starts here!

Every child learns to read in a different way and at his or her own speed. Some go back and forth between reading levels and read favorite books again and again. Others read through each level in order. You can help your young reader improve and become more confident by encouraging his or her own interests and abilities. From books your child reads with you to the first books he or she reads alone, there are I Can Read Books for every stage of reading:

SHARED READING
Basic language, word repetition, and whimsical illustrations, ideal for sharing with your emergent reader

BEGINNING READING
Short sentences, familiar words, and simple concepts for children eager to read on their own

READING WITH HELP
Engaging stories, longer sentences, and language play for developing readers

READING ALONE
Complex plots, challenging vocabulary, and high-interest topics for the independent reader

ADVANCED READING
Short paragraphs, chapters, and exciting themes for the perfect bridge to chapter books

I Can Read Books have introduced children to the joy of reading since 1957. Featuring award-winning authors and illustrators and a fabulous cast of beloved characters, I Can Read Books set the standard for beginning readers.

A lifetime of discovery begins with the magical words "I Can Read!"

Visit www.icanread.com for information
on enriching your child's reading experience.

Library of Congress Cataloging-in-Publication Data is available.

ISBN 978-0-06-186438-4 (trade bdg.) —ISBN 978-0-06-186437-7 (pbk.)

Typography by Sean Boggs

11 12 13   LP/WOR   10 9 8 7 6 5 4 3 2   ❖   First Edition

I Can Read!™

BEGINNING READING 1

DUCKS in a ROW

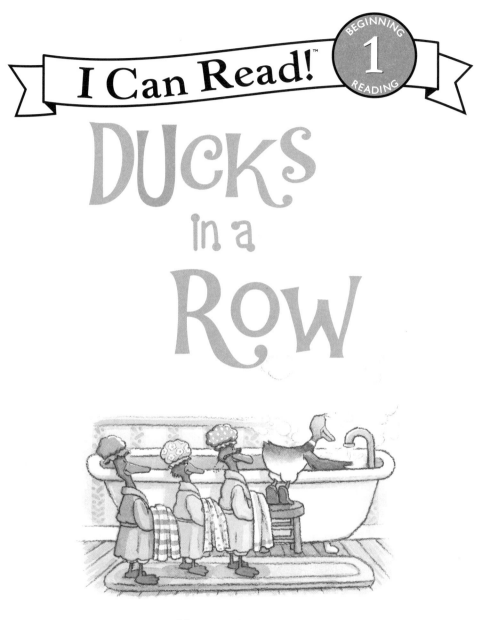

based on the bestselling books of
Jackie Urbanovic

story by Lori Haskins Houran

pictures by Joe Mathieu

HARPER

An Imprint of HarperCollinsPublishers

Max sat down.

He put up his feet.

He leaned back in his chair.

"Oh, yes," he said.

"It's nice to relax."

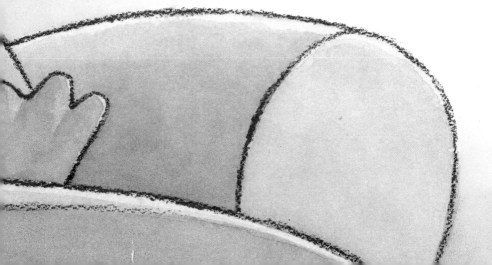

Max looked around.

Brody was bringing in the newspaper.

Dakota was warming Irene's feet.

Bebe was singing the kittens to sleep.

Everyone had something to do.

Everyone except him.

"Hmm," said Max.

"What do I do around here?"

Sometimes he baked snacks.

But he wondered if

everyone liked them.

8

"Does anyone need me
to do anything?" Max asked.
No one answered.

Just then the doorbell rang.

"I'll get it!" Max yelled.

On the step stood

three plump ducks in a row.

"Aunt Pat! Aunt Dot! Aunt Flo!"

said Max.

"Max, could you take my bag?"
said Aunt Pat.

"And my bundle?" said Aunt Dot.

"And my box?" said Aunt Flo.

"Of course!" said Max.

Max's aunts told everyone
they were on their way south.
They had stopped to visit
until the first snowfall.

The aunts sat down on the couch.

"Max, could you make some tea?"

said Aunt Pat.

"With toast?" said Aunt Dot.

"And jam?" said Aunt Flo.

Max set to work.

It felt good to be needed.

Lucky for Max,

the aunts needed him quite a bit.

They needed him to bring their books

and find their glasses.

They needed him to turn on their lamps.

They needed him to run their baths,

to fluff their pillows,

and to close their curtains.

By the end of the day,

Max was a little tired.

But it still felt good to be needed.

The next morning started early.

"Max, could you open this jar?"

said Aunt Pat.

"And untangle this yarn?"

said Aunt Dot.

"And fix this toaster?"

said Aunt Flo.

Beauty
Cream

The rest of the week,
all Max heard was
"Max, could you . . . "

"Turn on the TV?"

"Pop some popcorn?"

"Change the channel?"

"Shuffle the cards?"

"Roll the dice?"

"Keep the score?"

"Pick a pumpkin?"

"Pick an apple?"

"Pick some flowers?"

Max went out to the garden.

He wasn't sure how much more

being needed he could take!

Then he felt something.

A snowflake.

"The first snowfall!" he said.

The very next day Max said
good-bye to Aunt Pat,
Aunt Dot, and Aunt Flo.

He was so tired
he could hardly wave.

Max sat down.

He put up his feet.

He leaned back in his chair.

"Oh, yes," he said.

"It's nice to relax."

Then he heard Irene's voice.

"Max, could you . . ."

"Oh, no!" thought Max.

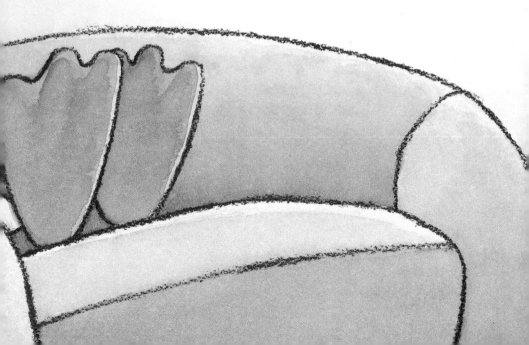

"Max, could you use a blanket?"
said Irene.

Max nodded.

And he fell fast asleep.